**W9-CHS-700**

DATE DUE

| | |
|---|---|
| | |
| | |
| | |
| | |
| | |
| | |
| | |
| | |
| | |
| | |
| | |
| | |
| | |
| | |
| | |
| | |
| | |

DEMCO, INC. 38-2931

# Popular Rock Superstars of Yesterday and Today

# POP ROCK

AC/DC

Aerosmith

The Allman
Brothers Band

The Beatles

Billy Joel

Bob Marley
and the Wailers

Bruce Springsteen

The Doors

Elton John

The Grateful Dead

Led Zeppelin

Lynyrd Skynyrd

Pink Floyd

Queen

The Rolling
Stones

U2

The Who

# Led Zeppelin

Ethan Schlesinger

Mason Crest Publishers

# Led Zeppelin

FRONTIS  Led Zeppelin (clockwise from left: Robert Plant, John Bonham, Jimmy
Page, John Paul Jones) has been one of the most influential bands in rock history.

Produced by 21st Century Publishing and Communications, Inc.

Editorial by Harding House Publishing Services, Inc.

MASON CREST PUBLISHERS INC.
370 Reed Road
Broomall, Pennsylvania 19008
(866) MCP-BOOK (toll free)
www.masoncrest.com

Printed in the United States.

First Printing

9 8 7 6 5 4 3 2 1

Library of Congress Cataloging-in-Publication Data

Schlesinger, Ethan.
    Led Zeppelin / Ethan Schlesinger.
       p. cm.—(Popular rock superstars of yesterday and today)
    Includes bibliographical references and index.
    Hardback edition: ISBN-13: 978-1-4222-0212-8
    Paperback edition: ISBN-13: 978-1-4222-0324-8
 1. Led Zeppelin (Musical group)—Juvenile literature. 2. Rock musicians—United
States—Biography—Juvenile literature. I. Title.
ML3930.L32S34 2008
782.42166092'2—dc22
[B]                                                    2007012142

# CONTENTS

# ROCK 'N' ROLL TIMELINE

**1951**
"Rocket 88," considered by many to be the first rock single, is released by Ike Turner.

**1952**
DJ Alan Freed coins and popularizes the term "Rock and Roll," proclaimes himself the "Father of Rock and Roll," and declares, "Rock and Roll is a river of music that has absorbed many streams: rhythm and blues, jazz, rag time, cowboy songs, country songs, folk songs. All have contributed to the Big Beat."

**1955**
"Rock Around the Clock" by Bill Haley & His Comets is released; it tops the U.S. charts and becomes wildly popular in Britain, Australia, and Germany.

**1967**
The Monterey Pop Festival in California kicks off open air rock concerts.

**1965**
The psychedelic rock band, the Grateful Dead, is formed in San Francisco.

**1969**
The Woodstock Music and Arts Festival attracts a huge crowd to rural upstate New York.

**1969**
*Tommy*, the first rock opera, is released by British rock band The Who.

**1970**
The Beatles break up.

**1971**
Jim Morrison, lead singer of The Doors, dies in Paris.

**1971**
Duane Allman, lead guitarist of the Allman Brothers Band, dies.

## 1950s          1960s          1970s

**1957**
Bill Haley tours Europe.

**1957**
Jerry Lee Lewis and Buddy Holly become the first rock musicians to tour Australia.

**1954**
Elvis Presley releases the extremely popular single "That's All Right (Mama)."

**1961**
The first Grammy for Best Rock 'n' Roll Recording is awarded to Chubby Checker for *Let's Twist Again*.

**1964**
The Beatles make their first visit to America, setting off the British Invasion.

**1969**
A rock concert held at Altamont Speedway in California is marred by violence.

**1969**
The Rolling Stones tour America as "The Greatest Rock and Roll Band in the World."

**1973**
*Rolling Stone* magazine names Annie Leibovitz chief photographer and "rock 'n' roll photographer;" she follows and photographs rockers Mick Jagger, John Lennon, and others.

**1974**
*Sheer Heart Attack* by the British rock band Queen becomes an international success.

**1974**
"Sweet Home Alabama" by Southern rock band Lynyrd Skynyrd is released and becomes an American anthem.

**1987**
Billy Joel becomes the first American rock star to perform in the Soviet Union since the construction of the Berlin Wall.

**2005**
Led Zeppelin is ranked #1 on VH1's list of the 100 Greatest Artists of Hard Rock.

**2005**
Many rock groups participate in Live 8, a series of concerts to raise awareness of extreme poverty in Africa.

**1985**
Rock stars perform at Live Aid, a benefit concert to raise money to fight Ethiopian famine.

**2003**
Led Zeppelin's "Stairway to Heaven" is inducted into the Grammy Hall of Fame.

**1980**
John Lennon of the Beatles is murdered in New York City.

**2000s**
Aerosmith's album sales reach 140 million worldwide and the group becomes the bestselling American hard rock band of all time.

**2007**
Billy Joel become the first person to sing the National Anthem before two Super Bowls.

**1975**
*Tommy*, the movie, is released.

**1975**
*Time* magazine features Bruce Springsteen on its cover as "Rock's New Sensation."

**1995**
The Rock and Roll Hall of Fame and Museum opens in Cleveland, Ohio.

# 1970s    1980s    1990s    2000s

**1979**
Pink Floyd's *The Wall* is released.

**1991**
Freddie Mercury, lead vocalist of the British rock group Queen, dies of AIDS.

**2004**
Elton John receives a Kennedy Center Honor.

**1979**
The first Grammy for Best Rock Vocal Performance by a Duo or Group is awarded to The Eagles.

**2004**
*Rolling Stone Magazine* ranks The Beatles #1 of the 100 Greatest Artists of All Time, and Bob Dylan #2.

**1986**
The Rolling Stones receive a Grammy Lifetime Achievement Award.

**1981**
MTV goes on the air.

**2006**
U2 wins five more Grammys, for a total of 22—the most of any rock artist or group.

**1986**
The first Rock and Roll Hall of Fame induction ceremony is held; Chuck Berry, Little Richard, Ray Charles, Elvis Presley, and James Brown, are among the first inductees.

**1981**
*For Those About to Rock We Salute You* by Australian rock band AC/DC becomes the first hard rock album to reach #1 in the U.S.

**2006**
Bob Dylan, at age 65, releases *Modern Times* which immediately rises to #1 in the U.S.

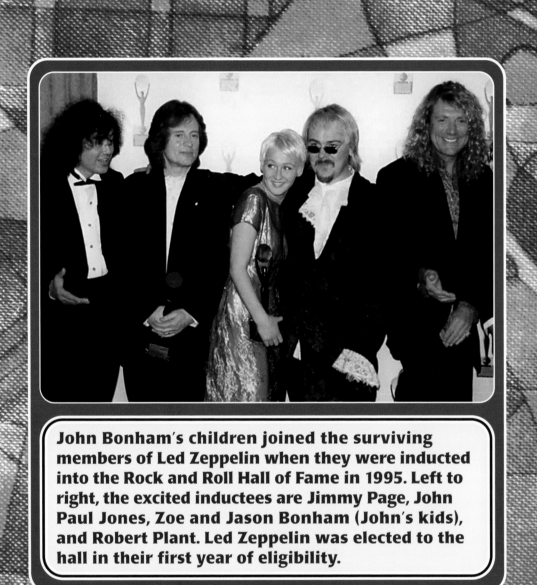

John Bonham's children joined the surviving members of Led Zeppelin when they were inducted into the Rock and Roll Hall of Fame in 1995. Left to right, the excited inductees are Jimmy Page, John Paul Jones, Zoe and Jason Bonham (John's kids), and Robert Plant. Led Zeppelin was elected to the hall in their first year of eligibility.

# 1

# "Ever Onward" to the Hall

It looks as though it could be part of the set for a sci-fi movie. The large, eight-story glass pyramid rises from the shore of Lake Erie. At first glance, it seems to stand alone. But closer inspection reveals it to be the entrance to the Rock and Roll Hall of Fame, designed by the famous architect I. M. Pei.

The pyramid leads to a futuristic building constructed of simple geometric shapes. According to the designer, who also designed such buildings as the Javits Convention Center in New York City and the Pyramide du Louvre in Paris, he wanted the structure to "express the **dynamic** music it celebrates." And in 1995, the hall welcomed one of the most dynamic groups in rock 'n' roll history—Led Zeppelin. Though the induction ceremony took place in January, it would not be until fall 1995 that the Rock and Roll Hall of Fame would be open to the public.

## Into the Hall

Getting into the Rock and Roll Hall of Fame is not a "given." Just because a person or group laid down some tracks in a recording studio doesn't mean a spot in the hall. Musicians such as Led Zeppelin must first be nominated by a committee of music experts. The nominating committee examines all potential nominees' credentials to determine if their names should be put on the ballot. The selection **criteria** includes the passage of at least twenty-five years since the individual's or group's first recording and the role the musicians played in the history and development of rock music.

The ballot containing the year's nominees is sent to a select group of music experts who vote on the musicians who will make it into the hall. To win election, the musician must receive at least 50 percent of the vote. In some cases, it takes many tries before a group makes it into the hall. For others, like Led Zeppelin, their influence is so obvious that they make it in on the first try.

## The Ceremony

As futuristic as the Rock and Roll Hall of Fame is, is how traditional— some might say old-fashioned—the ballroom of the Waldorf Astoria Hotel is. The New York City site has been the home of the hall's induction ceremonies since they began. The biggest names in the rock world are here, some dressed in suits and ties, some not. The ceremony and location seem unusual for some, including Neil Strauss of the *New York Times*:

> **"Rock music is supposed to be loud, rebellious and impulsive, and the notion of honoring it with a big, lavish party of tuxedo-clad record company executives seems antithetical to its original impulses. On the other hand, rock-and-roll has come a long way in the last half-century, evolving into one of the world's most popular and significant forms of music."**

On the evening of January 12, 1995, the tuxedo-clad crowd had gathered to see Led Zeppelin, the Allman Brothers Band, Al Green, Janis Joplin, Martha and the Vandellas, Neil Young, Frank Zappa, among others, take their places in the Rock and Roll Hall of Fame.

It was a night of serious music. Robert Plant, Jimmy Page, and John Paul Jones—the surviving members of Led Zeppelin—performed together for the first time in six years. Neil Young joined the guys for "When the Levee Breaks."

Aerosmith's Joe Perry and Steven Tyler, who had presented the group at the ceremony, joined Robert, Jimmy, and John Paul on

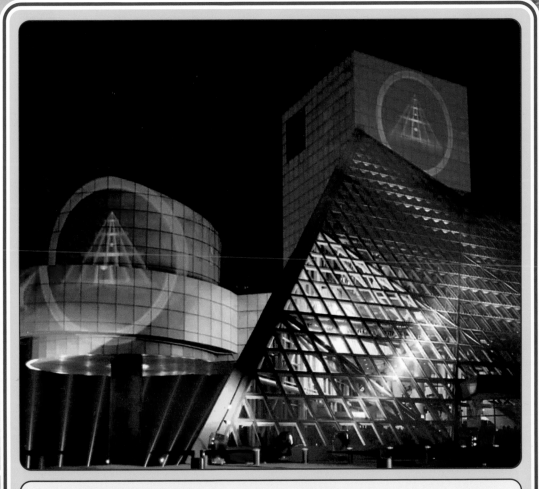

Though you might think you've walked onto a movie set or into a dream of what the world will look like in the future, you haven't. You're just in Cleveland, Ohio—at the Rock and Roll Hall of Fame and Museum on the shores of Lake Erie, where rock 'n' roll's stories and stars are memorialized.

**Joe Perry (left) and Steven Tyler (in the crazy hat) hang with Robert Plant and Jimmy Page at a party following the Rock and Roll Hall of Fame induction ceremony. The Aerosmith rockers had the honor of presenting Led Zeppelin for its induction. They also joined the inductees for a performance that got the audience out of its seats.**

"Bring It on Home," "Long Distance Call Blues," and "Baby Please Don't Go." Playing the drums for that set was Jason Bonham, the son of Led Zeppelin's late drummer John "Bonzo" Bonham. The age difference between the members of Led Zeppelin and Steve and Joe of Aerosmith and the young drummer was not missed by *New York Times* music critic Neil Strauss. He described the group as "five of them with long hair and wrinkles."

## Cheers and Jeers

Led Zeppelin's induction to the Rock and Roll Hall of Fame wasn't all words of praise and **accolades**. In his induction speech, Steven paid **homage** to Led Zeppelin's music philosophy; in 1977, Jimmy had declared the group's motto to be "Ever onward," and the group had persisted in pushing the envelope when it came to making their music. But, things had not always been rosy between Steven and at least one member of the group. Neil Strauss described part of Steven's induction speech:

> **"In introducing Led Zeppelin before their induction, Aerosmith's Mr. Tyler recalled the time he saw a woman he was living with walk out of a Led Zeppelin concert arm in arm with an amorous Mr. Page."**

Well, rock groups *did* have a reputation of hard living and womanizing (among other things)!

There was even tension between members of the group at this supposedly happy occasion. When John Paul accepted his award, he addressed John and Robert: "Thank you, my friends, for finally remembering my phone number." Jimmy and Robert had neglected to invite John Paul to participate in their reunion tour.

Despite the hard feelings between John Paul and the other surviving members of Led Zeppelin, it was a special night for them and for their particular flavor of rock music. That evening, they became the first hard rock band to enter the Rock and Roll Hall of Fame. The group's influence on rock music is widespread, as is the group that gave birth to Led Zeppelin—the Yardbirds.

When the four guys who make up Led Zeppelin finally got together, it seemed to be a match made in heaven. They might not have agreed about everything, but together their music was unstoppable. From the top left, John Bonham, Robert Plant, Jimmy Page, and John Paul Jones pose for an early photo.

# 2

# Things That Fly

**O**ne of the most successful bands in rock was also one of its first—Led Zeppelin. The group has reportedly sold more than 300 million albums. VH1 anointed the band the #1 greatest artist of hard rock. Though the band's reputation would be forever associated with hard rock, its formation began with a much softer sound.

## The Yardbirds

In the early days of British rock, there existed a band called the Yardbirds. The group began in 1962 as the Metropolitan Blues Quartet, and became well known in the London area for its bluesy sounds. The group took its influences from blues greats Howlin' Wolf, Muddy Waters, and Elmore James.

In 1963, the group's original guitarist was replaced by Eric Clapton. Though his guitar ability had not reached the virtuoso status to which it has since evolved, his talent was already evident in those early days. With Eric, the group began to develop a reputation as innovators in the use of the guitar in rock. The Yardbirds are credited with developing the guitar techniques of feedback, distortion, and better use of amplifiers. They were pioneers in using complex lead guitar parts, including solos, in their repertoire.

The Yardbirds are perhaps best known for who spent time playing guitar for the group, rather than for their group recordings. When Eric left (he didn't like the band's move toward a more pop-rock sound), he recommended Jimmy Page to replace him. Jimmy, however, had security as a studio musician. Working as a session musician, Jimmy had performed with Donovan, Them, the Kinks, and the Who, many of the musicians responsible for the **British Invasion** that hit the United States. He suggested Jeff Beck, who joined the band, but Jimmy's involvement with the group wasn't over.

## Jimmy and the Yardbirds

When the band's bass player decided to give up the guitar and become a record producer, members of the Yardbirds again contacted Jimmy about joining the group. This time he agreed, but only on a temporary basis. Jimmy agreed to play bass until another member of the band was comfortable with it. Eventually, Jimmy and Jeff began playing twin leads, to critical raves.

Whether he was fired or he resigned, Jeff left the group after a gig in Texas. Jimmy was now the group's only lead guitarist. By 1968, many of the group members were ready to slow down. They had been on an almost constant treadmill of recording and touring, and they were tired and wanted to try something new. In July, they played their last gig, and the Yardbirds were left to become a chapter of rock music history.

Almost. They had one gig left to play. The band had already signed a contract to play in Scandinavia. Jimmy was determined to fulfill the obligation, and set out to pull together a new band. Chris Dreja, who had been the Yardbirds' bass player, agreed to stay with Jimmy's new group. Their first choice for lead singer said no, but he recommended a singer named Robert Plant. In an interview with

One of the most important groups in the early days of British rock was the Yardbirds. They had a good sound and put out some hit records, but they are perhaps best known for rock legends such as Eric Clapton, Jeff Beck, and Jimmy Page (second from left) who spent time playing in the band.

Cameron Crowe, Jimmy spoke of his first impression of the blues singer from Birmingham:

“His vocal range was unbelievable. I thought, 'Wait a minute. There's something wrong here. He's not known.' I couldn't figure it out. I thought, 'he must be a strange guy or something.' Then he came over to my place and I could see that he was a really good guy. I still don't know why he hadn't made it yet." **"**

Robert agreed to join the group. He also suggested that they approach one of his former band mates, John "Bonzo" Bonham, to play the drums. John agreed, and the lineup was set until Chris decided he didn't want to play music anymore; he wanted to become a photographer. John Paul Jones's wife read an article in *Disc Magazine* about the new group and, at her insistence, John Paul contacted Jimmy about playing bass and keyboards. Jimmy had worked with John Paul when he was doing session work, so he was familiar with his work. John Paul's pedigree as a session musician was as impressive as Jimmy's. John Paul had played with such musicians as the Rolling Stones, Donovan, Jeff Beck, and Dusty Springfield. When John Paul joined Jimmy, John, and Robert, the group's membership was set for many years—though its name wasn't.

## Becoming Led Zeppelin

With Jimmy, John, Robert, and John Paul in sync, the guys fulfilled the Scandinavian commitments as the New Yardbirds. The band returned to Britain after the tour, ready to go into the recording studio to cut their first tracks. But first they had to do something about the name. Earlier, Keith Moon, who also played with the Yardbirds, had talked with Jimmy about forming a supergroup. Among the names discussed for that group, which was never to come about, Keith suggested Lead Zeppelin, which according to some sources came from another former Yardbird, John Entwistle. He used the term to describe a bad performance (going over like a lead zeppelin). Jimmy, John, Robert, and John Paul, liked it, but their manager, Peter Grant, insisted that the "a" be dropped in "Lead" so Americans wouldn't pronounce it "Leed."

Now Led Zeppelin, the group went into Olympic Studios to record. Although all the members were experienced musicians, for vocalist Robert, this was his first time in a full-service recording studio. He told Cameron Crowe:

"I'd go back to the playback room and listen. . . . It had so much weight, so much power, it was devastating. I had a long way to go with my voice then, but the enthusiasm and sparking of work with Jimmy's guitar . . . it was so raunchy. All these things, bit-by-bit, started fitting into a trademark for us."

Led Zeppelin drummer John "Bonzo" Bonham first joined the guys when Jimmy put together a new version of the Yardbirds. Robert Plant, already on board, convinced Jimmy that they should approach the talented drummer. Robert and John had played together in another rock band, and Robert was well aware of John's skills as a stick man.

When Jimmy first listened to Robert, he couldn't believe the sounds that came from the young musician's mouth. Because Robert wasn't hooked up with a group, Jimmy thought that perhaps Robert was strange. It turns out that the only thing strange about him was the uniqueness of his vocal talents.

Anxious to get their first recording out to the public, the band worked hard to finish the album. According to Robert:

**"We finished the album in three weeks. Jimmy invested all his Yardbirds money, which wasn't much, into our first tour. We took a road crew of one and off we went."**

## Meet Led Zeppelin

On October 15, 1968, Led Zeppelin played its first concert under that name. The show at Surrey University introduced the song "Dazed and Confused." Over the years, that song became **synonymous** with both the group and with Jimmy. At the suggestion of the father of David McCallum (an actor on the 1960s television show *Man from U.N.C.L.E.*, who since 2003, has played Dr. Donald "Ducky" Mallard on *NCIS*), who played the violin, Jimmy played part of his solo using a violin bow.

Led Zeppelin introduced itself in a series of concerts around Britain. Though fans were supportive, the music press was less impressed. Some music critics found things to like about the group, but many didn't see anything special about the newest band looking to make a dent in the music market.

What the British press didn't count on was the group's **savvy** manager, Peter Grant. He had, after all, convinced Atlantic Records to sign the band with what was then the largest advance paid to a rock band. This came though no executive from Atlantic had heard the band. The decision had been made based largely on the recommendation of Dusty Springfield and the persuasive power of the group's manager.

Peter paid close attention to what was happening on the U.S. music scene. He talked rock promoters into hiring the band to replace the Jeff Beck Group, which had cancelled several tour appearances. So on Christmas 1968, Led Zeppelin found itself in sunny California. Robert described the experience to Cameron:

**"We'd barely even been abroad, and here we were. It was the first time I saw a cop with a gun, the first time I saw a twenty-foot long car. The whole thing**

was a complete bowl-over. It was Christmas, and Christmas away from home for the English is the end of the world. I went wandering down the Sunset Strip with no shirt on. . . . We threw eggs, had silly water battles and had all the good fun that a 19-year-old boy should have. **"**

They might have been having fun, but the band was also there to work.

## The First Album

In early 1969, the band released *Led Zeppelin*. In a press kit for the album, Jimmy describes the group's music:

**"**Every one of us has been influenced by the blues, but it's one's interpretation of it and how to utilize it. I wish someone would invent an expression, but the closest I can get is contemporary blues.**"**

According to John Paul, the group was all about exploring music:

**"**We all had ideas, and we'd use everything we came across, whether it was folk, country music, blues, Indian, Arabic.**"**

No matter what label was slapped on the music, the album showed the influences of Delta blues and folk, but with a touch uniquely the group's own. Robert and Jimmy, for example, had their own version of call-and-response, popular in blues music; Jimmy played something on his guitar, and Robert mimicked it with his voice, sometimes almost screaming (or screeching).

The album reaches #10 on the album charts. Though popular with fans, it met with mixed reviews by the critics. One of the most important critics of the time, John Mendelsohn of the *Rolling Stone*, accused the group of stealing music, showing off, and copying black musicians—badly. The accusations so angered the band that for many years, they refused interviews with anyone associated with the magazine.

Led Zeppelin didn't have to wait long to taste success, and they took a big bite! Its first album was a huge hit with the fans. It was what music lovers had been wanting. By 1975, sales of the album had reached $7 million. *Rolling Stone* ranked the album #29 on its list of greatest albums in rock history.

*Rolling Stone*'s bad review wasn't the only problem the album caused the band. Jeff Beck accused the band of stealing his idea for recording "You Shook Me." This controversy ended the long-term friendship of Jimmy and Jeff.

## A Follow-Up and More Problems

*Rolling Stone* aside, Led Zeppelin's first album was a big success. In December 1969, the group's second album came out. *Led Zeppelin II*

**The group started in small clubs, but before long, Led Zeppelin was playing in some of the largest venues in the United States. American audiences welcomed with open arms the new band and its unique sound. And concertgoers knew they would get their money's worth, as the group's shows could go on for hours.**

reached #1 on the U.S. album charts and was a huge success. "Whole Lotta Love" became the band's first single to hit the top-40 charts, peaking at #4.

But, the album also brought problems. Several of the album's songs were very similar to ones published by Arc Music and released on Chess Records, the legendary blues label. Led Zeppelin was sued by Arc for copyright infringement for "Bring It on Home," which Arc said used a cover of Sonny Blake's song of the same name and was too similar to "Bring It on Back" by Willie Dixon; neither of these artists were credited. Eventually, the case was settled out of court in favor of Arc Music. Several years later, the band was sued by Willie over "Whole Lotta Love." Again, the case was settled out of court, with Led Zeppelin paying the musician a large amount of money.

## Getting Bigger—and Longer

The band became a big hit on the U.S. concert scene. In the beginning, it played clubs and other small **venues**, but it wasn't long before concerts had to move to larger sites. People who came to the concerts also quickly learned to come prepared for a long show. In many cases, the concerts stretched to more than three hours (one song could last forty-five minutes), much longer than most musicians were willing to perform.

In 1970, *Led Zeppelin III* was released. This album was more **acoustic** than the other ones. Although it became the group's second #1 album, this new sound wasn't as popular with critics or the fans.

In November of 1970, Atlantic released "Immigrant Song" as a single, without the group's permission. Led Zeppelin saw its albums as a whole, from which individual pieces should not be taken. AM radio concentrated on playing singles, and most of the songs were only two or three minutes long. Many of Led Zeppelin's songs ran much longer than that, so Atlantic released shortened versions. Despite the group's protests, nine singles were released.

The group and its manager felt strongly about how their music was presented, and they aimed for album-focused radio stations. Limited song length also meant that Led Zeppelin would have to edit its music to appear on most television programs. Rather than compromise its sound, the group decided to avoid appearing on television. For rock groups during the early 1970s, that was almost unheard of.

That wasn't the only difference Led Zeppelin had from other groups. Its concerts received little advertising. Fans used word of mouth to let each other know about performances, releases, and other band information. They considered themselves members of a very exclusive club—but one that would soon get much bigger.

Led Zeppelin quickly became the biggest band in the world, and fans everywhere eagerly awaited the next concert. But fame did have some downsides: constant travel, "grabby" fans, tight schedules, and little time to relax. But it also came with perks, like a private airplane to get the guys from performance to performance in comfort.

# 3

## "Biggest Band in the World"

Led Zeppelin's first three albums and frequent tours had made the group a formidable force in the United States. Now the group and Peter Grant looked to take over the music world. And they would be successful, at least in the first half of the 1970s. Led Zeppelin's fourth album would play a major role in the group's world domination.

### Album #4

Led Zeppelin's next album probably has more titles by which it's known than any other in rock history: *Led Zeppelin IV*, or *Runes, The Fourth Album*, or *ZOSO.* . . . The original album cover didn't have a title, only a series of runes, symbols that some believe have magical powers. In a 2005 interview with *Rolling Stone*, Robert said it was *The Fourth Album*.

Released in November 1971, the album—whatever its name—helped solidify Led Zeppelin's place in the rock world. It stayed on *Billboard*'s album charts for the next five years, peaking at #2.

The group was always willing to experiment, and this album shows a melding of folk music, blues, and hard rock. John's drum work is featured on "Rock and Roll." The song is a heavy-metal homage to the early days of rock. "When the Levee Broke" is Led Zeppelin's version of a blues number by Memphis Minnie/Kansas Joe McCoy. Again, the drum is featured, this time recorded in a stairwell to achieve the distinctive sound.

## Stairway to the Top

The best known song from *The Fourth Album*, however, is "Stairway to Heaven." Even non–Led Zeppelin fans know "she's buying a stairway to heaven." Jimmy had started working on the song by himself, but he played it for Robert, and the pair began working on it. According to Robert:

> **Yeah, I just sat next to Pagey while he was playing it through. It was done very quickly. It took a little working but, but it was a very fluid, unnaturally easy track. It was almost as if . . . it just had to be gotten out at that time. There was something pushing it, saying 'you guys are okay, but if you want to do something timeless, here's a wedding song for you.'**

In an interview in *Total Guitar*, he explained the lyrics this way:

> **My hand was writing our the words, 'There's a lady is sure [*sic*], all that glitters is gold, and she's buying a stairway to Heaven.' I just sat there and looked at them and almost leapt out of my seat. . . . [It was] a cynical aside about a woman getting everything she wanted all the time without giving back any thought or consideration. The first line begins with that cynical sweep of the hand . . . and it softened up after that.**

**Robert (left) and Jimmy (right) worked together closely on Led Zeppelin's big hit "Stairway to Heaven." Robert says the song seemed to come naturally, as though it was being given to the group. It was a nice present. The song's popularity continues today, more than thirty years after it was recorded.**

The song has become a classic. At one time, it was the most-played track in radio history, though the eight-minute song was never released as a single. According to *Total Guitar*, the sheet music to the song is the biggest selling ever, selling an average of 15,000 copies each year. A blend of folk and metal, Jimmy's solo has become legendary.

The song is not without controversy though. Almost since the beginning of rock, there have been attempts to find satanic and off-color messages and phrases in rock songs, usually when they are played backward. In the case of "Stairway to Heaven," the **allegations** were apparently first raised in a 1982 radio sermon. Others claim that in addition to the hidden messages, the lyrics themselves hold hidden meanings. At first, Led Zeppelin and its record company thought it best to ignore such allegations, hoping they would simply go away. But in a later interview with J. D. Considine, Robert finally spoke up:

> **"To me it's very sad, because 'Stairway to Heaven' was written with every best intention, and as far as reversing tapes and putting messages on the end, that's not my idea of making music."**

## A New Album, New Controversy, More Success

In 1973, Led Zeppelin released *Houses of the Holy*. Again controversy surrounded the group, this time for the choice of a record cover. The cover featured the images of nude children climbing in the direction of an idol. Some countries banned the sale of the album because of the cover image.

Many of the songs on the *Houses of the Holy* album were longer than ones on earlier albums. The band also made more use of **synthesizers** on the album, another trend of the era's hard rock music. Ironically, one of the songs not included on the album is "Houses of the Holy" although it was recorded. "Houses of the Holy" wouldn't make it onto an album for another two years.

Led Zeppelin was getting used to its albums hitting the top of the charts, and *Houses of the Holy* did not disappoint. The supporting tour broke attendance records at almost every stop. The group's Tampa, Florida, concert broke the attendance and receipt record set by the Beatles in 1965. Concert promoters began to book the band into bigger and bigger stadiums, and Led Zeppelin sold out most of them.

## Bad Boys

For most of its career, Led Zeppelin had prided itself on its lack of publicity. It had depended on fans to spread the word about the

Led Zeppelin, its music, and the number of its fans kept growing until the group's concerts had to be held in major stadiums. Concert attendance figures broke records all over North America—including a record set by the Beatles, one of the hottest groups of the time. An empty seat at a Led Zeppelin concert was rare.

group's albums and concerts, and the fans enjoyed the special closeness that implied. Unfortunately, by 1973 that secrecy had begun to work against the group. Despite the sellout concerts and huge album sales, photos of other bands were showing up on magazine covers and getting all the publicity. Led Zeppelin, one of the rare groups not to have a publicist, found itself playing second-fiddle in press coverage to other British groups such as the Rolling Stones and the Who.

It wasn't that the group was getting no publicity in the press. The problem actually was that it was getting the wrong kind of

**The band worked hard, there was no doubt about that. But the members of Led Zeppelin enjoyed themselves as well. When Robert (left) and Jimmy (right) performed, they put their hearts and souls into it. They had fun, too, and the audience could tell they enjoyed performing. No one says work can't be fun!**

press coverage. When stories about the group did make the press, they often were tales of riots over concert tickets and motorcycle rides through hotel hallways. According to one well-circulated story, John threw television sets out a hotel window and blamed it on groupies.

## Swan Song

In 1974, Led Zeppelin decided to set up its own record label. Of course they'd record on the label, but it would also release recordings by other groups.

The group released its first album on Swan Song in February 1975. *Physical Graffiti*, a double album, featured new cuts as well as tracks that had been recorded in previous years but not released on previous albums. *Rolling Stone* reviewed the album and called it a "bid for artistic respectability."

It was another huge success for the group and reached #1 on the charts in only its second week of release. The success of the album as well as the supporting tour brought the re-release of all of the previously released Led Zeppelin's albums. On March 25, 1975, Led Zeppelin became the first group in history to have six albums on the charts at the same time.

## Difficult and Sad Times

By 1975, there could be no question that Led Zeppelin was a huge factor in rock music. Not many groups then (or since) had achieved the success of Led Zeppelin. Unfortunately, the latter half of the 1970s wasn't such a high ride.

In August of 1975, Robert and his wife were traveling in Greece. Their car went over a cliff, and his wife suffered a skull fracture and a broken leg and pelvis; she almost died. Robert fractured his elbow and broke his ankle.

Even in a small Greek hospital, Robert saw—or rather heard—evidence of Led Zeppelin's popularity:

**"I was lying there in some pain, trying to get cockroaches off the bed and the guy next to me, this drunken soldier, started singing 'The Ocean' from *Houses of the Holy*."**

For more than a year, it was uncertain whether Robert would be able to use his leg again. He spent the time drinking and playing the piano. But Jimmy, John, and John Paul knew that the group had to cut an album. Things moved quickly in the record industry, and Led Zeppelin needed a successful album to avoid becoming rock has-beens.

*Presence* was released during the spring of 1976 to mixed critical and fan response. Though the album went **platinum**, it was considered by many to be a disappointment. Some blamed the band's lackluster performance on the album to Jimmy's drug use; he began using heroin during work on the album.

## A Year They Should Have Skipped

The band was finally able to resume touring in 1977. It had been two years since Led Zeppelin had toured, and the band and its fans were more than ready for a dose of Zeppelin.

The tour was a huge success. Jimmy explained how the group seemed to work so well together during this tour:

> **The fact is that it's like a chemical fusion. . . . It sounds pretentious, but it's true. That's just what it is. When there are three people on stage, instrumentally, and I'm in the middle of a staccato thing, and Bonzo just for some unknown reasons happens to be there doing the same beats on the snare drum . . . that sort of thing is definitely a form of trans-state . . . it is a sort of communication on that other plane.**

Despite the almost ESP-like communication between group members that caused the tour's success, there was something different about this one. Problems seemed to follow the group on the tour. A riot broke out in Tampa, Florida, when a storm forced the band to end the concert early. Police officers used tear gas to break up the crowd, but not before several arrests and injuries occurred. John and members of the band's road crew were arrested after the first night of a stand in Oakland, California.

The next night, following the second concert of the Oakland stand, word came that Robert's son Karac, just five years old, had

The guys release an album: it's a big hit. The guys tour: they're a big hit. That was the life of Led Zeppelin in the mid-1970s. At one time they had six albums on charts at once. The group was big, and it looked as though things could only get bigger.

died from a viral infection. Devastated, the band returned to England, never to perform live in the United States again. Robert retreated to his country home, leaving the other members to worry about both him and the future of the group.

## Back in the Saddle

It took time, but Robert came back, eager to get back together with Jimmy, John, and John Paul. In late 1978, the group began working on *In Through the Out Door*. In the United States, the album became the

# LED ZEPPELIN

## A CRITICAL REVIEW OF THE BAND'S ROOTS AND BRANCHES

Even the biggest rock band in the world needs a break now and then. For Led Zeppelin, one of those breaks came when Robert's young son died. But the group was more than four guys working together. They were a family, and after taking the time to allow all of them to grieve, they were back in the studio.

first rock album to debut on *Billboard's* album chart at #1. "All My Love" was a Robert's tribute to his son.

Music trends were changing. Disco and punk were increasing in popularity, often pushing out the hard rock bands that had reigned supreme just a few years before. The group tried to accommodate some of those changes on its latest album. As a result, this was another album that was met with mixed reviews from fans and critics.

Jimmy, John, Robert, and John Paul were not ready for the rocker retirement home, however. In August 1979, they played at the prestigious Knebworth Music Festival to an estimated 420,000 screaming fans. If the band had wondered if it were losing its fans, Knebworth put to bed any doubts about the group's staying power.

## Good-Bye to the Stick Man

In 1980, the band undertook their first European tour in almost three years. The tour wasn't flashy, but it was successful. After the European leg, the group began rehearsals for another U.S. tour. Then disaster struck again.

One morning, when John Paul went to wake John, he found the thirty-two-year-old drummer dead. John had spent much of the previous night drinking, one of his favorite pastimes. After passing out, he had vomited. Because of the way he was lying, he had **asphyxiated**.

Once again, the band members were devastated by a death, this time in its immediate family. Naturally, the question arose about whether the group would go on. According to Jimmy:

> **❝It was impossible to continue, really. . . . Especially in light of what we'd done live, stretching and moving the songs this way and that. At that point in time . . . there was no way one wanted to even consider taking on another drummer. For someone to 'learn' the things Bonham had done . . . it just wouldn't have been honest. We had a great respect for each other, and that needed to continue . . . in life or death.❞**

Would Led Zeppelin survive this latest blow? The band's first answer was no.

What would be the best way to remember their bandmate and friend John "Bonzo" Bonham? It was a question Robert, John Paul, and Jimmy had to ask individually and as a group. After a while, the answer seemed obvious: they'd go on. For a tribute song, Jimmy added a little "spice" to a tune John had recorded.

# Together Again

**A**lthough the surviving members of Led Zeppelin were sure they couldn't go on without John, fans weren't so ready to let go of the band they loved so much. The group's fans hoped the end wasn't really the end, just a pause. It would take two years, but Led Zeppelin's fans would be rewarded for their patience.

When musicians go into the recording studio to lay down tracks for an album or CD, not all the songs may make it to that particular recording. This was true of Led Zeppelin, and *Coda*, released in 1982, featured songs previously recorded but not released. John's work was featured in an instrumental originally recorded in 1976. Jimmy added an extra "electronic" touch, and titled the song "Bonzo's Montreux."

The success of *Coda* led to the release in subsequent years of several box sets. The box sets were also snapped up by Zeppelin fans, and the group's popularity never **waned**.

## On Their Own

The group was releasing music, but it wasn't really *making* music. Jimmy, John Paul, and Robert made no real attempts to get back together in those early years after John's death. Instead, each member embarked on his own projects.

In 1983, Jimmy participated in the ARMS (Action Research for Multiple Sclerosis) Project. The tour brought together three of rock's greatest guitarists, and Yardbird alumni; besides Jimmy, Eric Clapton and Jeff Beck were part of the tour. The following year, Jimmy hooked up with Paul Rodgers of Bad Company to form the group the Firm. They released two albums, to a mediocre reception.

Robert performed as a solo artist as well. In 1982, he released *Pictures at Eleven.* The album was a critical and commercial success. He joined forces with Jimmy and Jeff Beck in 1984 and released *The Honeydrippers: Volume One.* Like Robert's solo efforts, this was also extremely popular with fans, though not quite as well received by critics.

As for John Paul, after Led Zeppelin broke up, he returned to his roots as a session musician. Even while playing with the group, he had kept his hand in session work, but with the group's end, he was able to spend more time playing bass and keyboards for other musicians, including R.E.M., Ben E. King, the Foo Fighters, and Paul McCartney. He also worked as a record producer.

## Live Aid

In the 1980s, the African country of Ethiopia was devastated by famine. In 1985, Bob Geldof of the Boomtown Rats decided to do something to help: he organized the mother of all rock concerts, Live Aid. Featuring some of the biggest names in rock, the July 13 concerts were held in Philadelphia and London, as well as in Sydney, Australia, and Moscow. Using some of the most up-to-date satellite transmission equipment, millions all over the world were able to see the concert and contribute to famine relief.

Live Aid was full of highlights, including now-classic performances by U2 and Queen. One of the lowlights, however, was the reunion of Led Zeppelin, who played in Philadelphia. With Phil Collins and Tony Thompson playing drums, Zeppelin performed "Rock and Roll," "Whole Lotta Love," and their classic "Stairway

Like the others, Robert didn't rest on his Led Zeppelin laurels. He also made a name for himself working with other artists and as a solo performer. This ad was used to announce Robert's solo album *Now and Zen*, which was released in 1988. Robert's albums were big hits with his fans.

to Heaven." Unfortunately, out-of-tune guitars, poor vocals, and drummers who lacked familiarity with the material weren't helped by technical difficulties in the broadcast. The group had no delusions about the quality of its performance; when a Live Aid anniversary DVD set was released in 2004, Robert, Jimmy, and John Paul refused to allow their set to be included in the concert footage.

But not everyone felt the group's performance was all bad. Cameron Crowe found memorable moments in Led Zeppelin's contribution to the concert:

> **"I'll remember Page's smile when Robert sang his familiar added-line to 'Stairway to Heaven'—'does anybody remember laughter.' It was a look that came from way down deep, and it carried with it a memory of a hundred Zeppelin shows gone by."**

## Does It Mean Reunion?

Fans anxious for the return of Led Zeppelin hoped that its Live Aid performance was just the first sign of an official group reunion. Though there wasn't much evidence of a reunion immediately after the concert disappointment, rumors began to fly again in 1988. Robert and Jimmy began performing on each other's solo albums. During solo concerts, Robert began incorporating tried-and-true Led Zeppelin songs along with new material for the first time. Jimmy joined Robert on stage to perform several concerts. The two also performed solo concert tours in the United States in late 1988. Both musicians' concerts were peppered with Led Zeppelin songs, stirring in the hearts of fans more hopes of a group reunion.

In May, Led Zeppelin again reunited to perform at the concert celebrating the fortieth anniversary of Atlantic Records. This time, Jason Bonham, John's son, was on the drums.

Though that performance and follow-up performances by Jason, Jimmy, and Robert fueled rumors of a reunion tour, nothing came about. Jimmy and Robert continued to perform on each other's recordings and even appear together in person, but for the most part, John Paul was not a part of those musical events. Then, in 1994, things came to a head, and the question of a reunion was finally answered.

A good cause reunited Led Zeppelin in 1985 when the guys performed at Live Aid, a series of concerts to raise money for famine relief. Unfortunately, their performance wasn't nearly as good as their intentions. The group refused to give permission for its performance to be included when the concert was released on DVD.

## So Long John Paul

After combined performances and joint recordings, Jimmy and Robert appeared on the hit show *MTV Unplugged*, in an episode called "Unledded." They were such a hit that it was only natural that talk of a reunion tour would again surface. The performance did lead to a world tour, but one composed of a rather unexpected backup band: a Middle Eastern orchestra! The group released a live album of the tour, *No Quarter*.

HALL OF FAME SPECIAL

*Rolling Stone*

ISSUE 702 • FEBRUARY 23, 1995 • $2.50

The Second Coming
**Led Zeppelin's**
Robert Plant & Jimmy Page
Candlebox's Teen Torch Songs
Pearl Jam's Pirate Radio
Slash's Snakepit • Soul Asylum

Robert (left) and Jimmy (right) found themselves on the cover of *Rolling Stone* magazine in 1995. The cover story talked about the reunion of Led Zeppelin. Funny thing, though: someone forgot to tell John Paul. Why? No one who knows is saying, and John Paul says he doesn't know. He read about the tour in the newspaper.

John Paul was nowhere to be found on the tour or album. Instead, Robert's son-in-law (and a member of his solo band), Charlie Jones, was on bass. Why? No one has been willing to say. In an interview with Dominick Miserandino on www.thecelebritycafe.com, when he was asked what happened, John Paul responded:

> **"I don't know. It was Page/Plant, you're right. They decided to do something on their own. . . . No, they didn't call me. I suppose they didn't have to. But they could have called me to tell me what they were doing . . . because they had to know people would call it a Zeppelin reunion, regardless of whether that's what they intended or not. They might have just warned me that it would be in the papers."**

That's how John Paul found out about the "reunion of sorts." He read about the tour in the newspaper.

The three surviving members of the group, however, were reunited—if only briefly—in 1995, when the group was inducted into the Rock and Roll Hall of Fame.

## More Zeppelin

In 1997, *Led Zeppelin BBC Sessions* was released and immediately became a hit. The following year, Robert and Jimmy released *Walking into Clarksdale*, which contained the pair's first album of all-new material since the end of Led Zeppelin. The supporting tour, however, featured mostly Zeppelin classics with a few of the new songs thrown in. Still, it and the album were hits.

Whether Robert and Jimmy or Led Zeppelin, by 1999, it was clear to everyone that fans wanted their Zeppelin.

rollingstone.com
Issue 1006 >> August 10, 2006 >> $3.95

# Rolling Stone

**LED ZEPPELIN**

## THE HEAVIEST BAND OF ALL TIME

Metal, Black Magic and Sex

**SPORTS ON THE EDGE**
The Craziest Extreme Stars

**THE ECO-RADICALS**
The Fall of the Violent Greens

1946-2006
**SYD BARRETT**
Floyd's Mad Genius

Robert (left) and Jimmy (right) found themselves on the cover of *Rolling Stone* again in 2006, when Led Zeppelin was rated "The Heaviest Band of All Time." Though the photo was of the most recent incarnation of the group, the honor also included John Paul and John Bonham. The story reflected the importance Led Zeppelin has had on rock music.

# The Zeppelin Legacy

L ed Zeppelin is a rare bird in the rock world. Most groups have a few years of hits and fame, but then disappear into **obscurity**. Their music might show up on a list of nostalgic songs, or they might be featured in a musical "walk down memory lane." But Zeppelin's music has not ever been out of **vogue**.

As the 1990s became the 2000s, Led Zeppelin was still popular. Some radio stations even had special blocks during which they played nothing but Led Zeppelin songs. The group's importance to the rock scene has become apparent during the new century as awards and tributes have come to the group.

## The Beginning of the New Millennium

As the new decade and new century began, Robert and Jimmy continued to perform together. And by 2002, there were even rumors that Robert and

John Paul were going to mend fences, paving the way for John Paul to rejoin Jimmy and Robert for a grand Led Zeppelin reunion tour in 2003. But the rumors were just that—rumors—and John Paul has remained estranged from Jimmy and Robert, except for when they *have* to be together. He told Dominick Miserandino;

> **"We keep it on a business basis, a professional basis. I deal with what I have to deal with concerning them. And I haven't really asked them about it. . . . I didn't really, care, you know?"**

John Paul has spent the first years of the new century recording solo albums, touring, playing sessions with musicians such as the Foo Fighters, and being a record producer. He also established his own recording studio and is involved in his daughter Jacinda's music career.

Jimmy and Robert released a live album in 2003, and Jimmy and Robert were the subjects of increased popularity. *Led Zeppelin DVD* was also released in 2003, and fans, many too young to have experienced the group's early days, had the opportunity to see the group when it was whole—complete with John Paul and John "Bonzo" Bonham. By December 2003, the DVD alone had sold more than a half a million copies. Not bad for a group whose lead members were now nearing sixty years of age, older than many of the fans' parents!

## Awards and Recognition

In the early twenty-first century, Led Zeppelin also found itself the recipient of many awards in recognition of its contribution to rock music. "Stairway to Heaven" was inducted into the Grammy Hall of Fame in 2003. In December 2004, "Stairway to Heaven" was voted the best rock song in history by listeners of the Planet Rock radio station. In 2005, the group received recognition by the Grammys, when they received the prestigious Grammy Lifetime Achievement Award. That same year, VH1 ranked Led Zeppelin #1 on its list of 100 Greatest Artists of Hard Rock. *Guitar World* magazine readers voted Jimmy's solo in "Stairway to Heaven" as the greatest guitar solo in all rock history.

John Paul's music career didn't end when Jimmy and Roger left him out of the new version of Led Zeppelin. In this photo, John Paul is shown performing solo in Germany. He's also done session work with other artists and produced records at his own recording studio. His daughter has a budding music career.

More awards followed in 2006. Along with Russian conductor Valery Gergiev, Led Zeppelin was awarded the 2006 Polar Music Prize. Jimmy, Robert, and John Paul, along with John's daughters, accepted the award from King Carl Gustav XVI of Sweden. The cover of the February 2006 *Guitar World* magazine declares Led Zeppelin the "world's greatest band." A poll of its readers proclaimed *Led Zeppelin IV* the greatest guitar album of all time in October. In 2006, the group was elected to the UK Music Hall of Fame.

Early 2007 also brought recognition to the group's music. It was announced that "Whole Lotta Love" would be added to the Grammy Hall of Fame.

Jimmy has also found himself the recipient of numerous accolades, mostly for his work as a member of Led Zeppelin. In 2003, *Rolling Stone* magazine ranked him #9 in its list of the greatest guitarists of all time. Guitar historian Robert Lynch describes Jimmy's guitar ability:

**"In the relatively short history of the electric guitar in rock music, there have been few who can be labeled as 'iconic.' Mr. Page is one of those select few. His eclectic stylings, his compositional prowess, his studio mastery and innovation, and his stage presentation were all areas where he excelled like no other and foreshadowed many who have followed in his wake."**

In 2005, Jimmy was awarded the Order of the British Empire in recognition of the charity work he does for many Brazilian charities, including the Action for Brazil's Children Trust, a charity established by his wife. Later that same year, Jimmy was made an honorary citizen of Rio de Janiero.

## Tributes

There's a cliché that imitation is the sincerest form of flattery. And that might indeed be true in the case of Led Zeppelin. In recognition of the group's importance in rock's history, many musicians have covered their songs. Most rock historians believe that one of the first musicians to cover a Led Zeppelin song was Sandie Shaw. In 1969,

**Jimmy's flying fingers helped make Led Zeppelin a rock 'n' roll phenomenon. Those fingers—and the rest of his hands too—were memorialized in cement on the Walk of Fame in London in 2004. *Rolling Stone* also recognized his talent, naming him the ninth-greatest guitarist in rock history. You can also now call him Sir Jimmy Page.**

she covered "Your Time Is Gonna Come." But Shaw was just the beginning. Tina Turner, Jeff Buckley, Nirvana, Iron Maiden, The Bobs, the Beastie Boys, Frank Zappa, Great White, Prince, Phish, and even the London Philharmonic Orchestra have covered or sampled from the Led Zeppelin songbook.

Other musicians have chosen to parody Led Zeppelin songs. When a song is parodied, it is copied in a funny way. One of the most famous parodies of a Led Zeppelin song is "Stairway to Gilligan's Island." The song was released in 1978 by Little Roger and the Goosebumps, a group out of Davis, California. The group shortened and adapted the words of "Stairway to Heaven" and put them to the music of the *Gilligan's Island*'s theme song. Thanks to its frequent appearance on the playlist of the "Dr. Demento Radio Show," a popular, nationally syndicated radio program, "Stairway to Gilligan's Island" became hugely popular with listeners. Though it might have been popular

If you're good, people want to copy you. If you're really good—like Led Zeppelin—people *really* want to copy you. And there are a lot of groups that want to honor Led Zeppelin by being a tribute band. One of the more common ones is ZoSo, shown in this photo.

with the public, representatives of Led Zeppelin weren't crazy about the song. They took those responsible for "Stairway to Gilligan's Island" to court, and copies of the song were pulled from sale.

Some groups go beyond simply covering or parodying Led Zeppelin's songs; they become tribute bands, choosing to perform the band's music under a name that is easily associated with that of the original group. Some of Led Zeppelin's tribute bands are the Music of Led Zeppelin, which played with the Minnesota Orchestra in 2006; Led Zepplica; Fred Zeppelin; and Dread Zeppelin, who performs Led Zeppelin songs reggae style complete with an Elvis Presley impersonator singing Robert Plant's leads.

## Keeping Control

Many musicians license their music for use in films, on television, in ads, or for release by other musicians. Obviously this brings in money to those who own the rights to the songs, but it can also increase interest in the original version of the song. However, licensing can be detrimental when rights are given to what might seem like almost anyone who asks and for whatever purpose.

For most of its existence, Led Zeppelin has bucked that trend. It has seldom allowed its music to be used for films, television, and other popular outlets for other musicians. As late as 2006, it was impossible to legally download Led Zeppelin songs from popular online music sites. Led Zeppelin wanted to keep control of how its music was used.

Led Zeppelin has begun to relax its restrictions, and the group is gaining new fans as a result. The group's fan base might not be growing significantly because of the use of "Rock and Roll" in Cadillac ads, but movies like *Almost Famous* and *School of Rock*, both of which feature the group's music, introduce a new generation to Zeppelin's sound.

## And Moving On

Though Led Zeppelin, for all intents and purposes, no longer exists, fans are still hopeful that group members will let bygones be bygones and reunite. In a BBC interview in 2006, Jimmy said "there will be some Zeppelin things on the horizon," fueling the hopes of the group's fans. In the meantime, the surviving members of Led Zeppelin have been busy on their own.

**Some of the guys in Led Zeppelin are old enough to be the fathers (or even grandfathers!) of many individuals who now make up the group's audiences and who buy its CDs and DVDs. Pennsylvania's Steve Sauer is a huge Led Zeppelin fan and runs a Web site dedicated to the band.**

John Paul continues touring and producing. Between 2004 and 2007, he worked on a new album. Eventually, he admitted that it was "coming slowly," perhaps one of rock's greatest understatements!

Robert has been recording and touring. His new group, Strange Sensation, has earned four Grammy nominations, but so far no wins. Robert's plans for 2007 had included the follow-up to *The Honeydrippers: Volume One*, which was recorded in 1984. However, the death of Atlantic Records co-founder Ahmet Ertegun in

December 2006 put those plans on hold, though Robert still hopes to record and release the CD.

Jimmy remains busy as well. He is spearheading efforts to remaster the Led Zeppelin catalog and still performs at charity events. He has played guitar for Sean Combs and performed with Fred Durst of Limp Bizkit at the 2001 European Video Music Awards. Jimmy has also said that he is planning to release a CD in 2007.

In January 2007, Jimmy was ranked #19 on Channel 4's list of The Ultimate Hellraiser. The list was intended to showcase the lifestyle many believed characterized rock music. The British show emphasized Jimmy's relationship with the band's many groupies, but nothing about his drug use; it also blamed Jimmy for many of John's more outrageous escapades, including his infamous hotel motorcycle ride.

To become a classic, a band, or at least its music, must have longevity. And few bands have had the long-lasting success of Led Zeppelin. Though the group disbanded decades ago, its music is still played regularly on radio stations all over the world. The band, as a whole and individually, is still earning awards for its music and performances. Each year the group gains more fans. Led Zeppelin fans—young and not so young—continue to hold out hope that Jimmy, Robert, and John Paul will reunite and come out with more of the sounds that have made Led Zeppelin a true classic of rock music.

**1962** The Yardbirds, which will play a significant role in the formation of Led Zeppelin, is formed as the Metropolitan Blues Quartet.

**1968** Jimmy forms a new band, which includes future Led Zeppelin members, to fulfill the Yardbirds' commitments.

**October 15** Led Zeppelin plays its first concert under that name.

**1969** The band releases its first album, *Led Zeppelin*.

Sandie Shaw covers "Your Time is Gonna Come," which most rock historians believe is the first cover of a Led Zeppelin song.

**December** The group's releases its second album, *Led Zeppelin II*.

**1970** *Led Zeppelin III* is released.

**November** Atlantic releases "Immigrant Song" as a single, without the group's permission.

**1971** **November** *Led Zeppelin IV* is released and will stay on the album charts for five years.

**1973** Led Zeppelin releases *Houses of the Holy*, with its controversial cover.

**1974** Led Zeppelin forms its own record label, Swan Song.

**1975** **March 25** Led Zeppelin becomes the first group in history to have six albums on the charts at the same time.

**August** Robert and his wife are seriously injured in a car accident in Greece.

**1977** Led Zeppelin resumes touring.

Robert's son Karac dies.

**1979** **August** The group plays at the Knebworth Music Festival.

**1980** Led Zeppelin goes on its first European tour in three years.

**September 25** John "Bonzo" Bonham dies.

**December 4** The surviving members of Led Zeppelin release a statement saying they are disbanding the group.

**1982** Allegations are first made that there are satanic references in "Stairway to Heaven."

Robert releases a solo effort, *Pictures at Eleven*.

**1983** Jimmy participates in the ARMS Project.

**1984** Jimmy joins with Paul Rodgers to form The Firm.

Robert, Jimmy, and Jeff Beck release *The Honeydrippers, Volume One.*

**1985** The surviving members of Led Zeppelin play at Live Aid.

**1988** Robert and Jimmy begin performing on each other's solo albums.

**1995** Led Zeppelin is inducted into the Rock and Roll Hall of Fame.

**1997** *Led Zeppelin BBC Sessions* is released and immediately becomes a hit.

**1998** Robert and Jimmy release *Walking into Clarksdale,* which contained the pair's first album of all-new material since the end of Led Zeppelin.

**2003** Jimmy and Robert release a live album.

"Stairway to Heaven" is inducted into the Grammy Hall of Fame.

*Rolling Stone* magazine ranks Jimmy Page #9 in its list of the greatest guitarists of all time.

**2004** **December** "Stairway to Heaven" is voted the best rock song in history by listeners of the Planet Rock radio station.

**2005** Led Zeppelin receives the prestigious Grammy Lifetime Achievement Award.

VH1 ranks Led Zeppelin #1 on its list of 100 Greatest Artists of Hard Rock.

*Guitar World* magazine readers vote Jimmy's solo in "Stairway to Heaven" as the greatest guitar solo in all rock history.

**2006** Led Zeppelin is awarded the Polar Music Prize.

The group is elected to the UK Music Hall of Fame.

**February** The cover of the February 2006 *Guitar World* magazine declares Led Zeppelin the "world's greatest band."

**2007** "Whole Lotta Love" is added to the Grammy Hall of Fame.

## Albums

**1969**  *Led Zeppelin*
       *Led Zeppelin II*

**1970**  *Led Zeppelin III*

**1971**  *Led Zeppelin IV*

**1973**  *Houses of the Holy*

**1975**  *Physical Graffiti*

**1976**  *Presence*
       *The Song Remains the Same*

**1979**  *In Through the Out Door*

**1982**  *Coda*

**1990**  *Led Zeppelin (Box Set, Vol. 1)*
       *Remasters*

**1993**  *The Complete Studio Recordings*
       *Led Zeppelin (Box Set, Vol. 2)*

**1997**  *BBC Sessions*

**1999**  *Early Days: The Best of Led Zeppelin Volume One*

**2000**  *Latter Days: The Best of Led Zeppelin Volume Two*

**2003**  *How the West Was Won*

## Number-One Singles

**1979**  "Fool in the Rain"

**1980**  "South Bound Suarez"

## Videos

**1976**  *The Song Remains the Same*

**2003**  *Led Zeppelin*

**2005**  *Inside Led Zeppelin: 1968–1980*
       *Led Zeppelin "The Story so Far"/The Lost Interviews*

**2006**  *Led Zeppelin: The Definitive Review*
*Live at Earls Court 1975*
*Origin of the Species*

**2007**  *In Their Own Words*
*Led Zeppelin: Way Down Inside*

## Awards and Recognition

**1995**  Inducted into the Rock and Roll Hall of Fame.

**2003**  Grammy Hall of Fame: "Stairway to Heaven" is inducted into the Grammy Hall of Fame; *Rolling Stone*: Jimmy Page is ranked #9 in its list of the greatest guitarists of all time.

**2004**  Planet Rock: "Stairway to Heaven" is voted the best rock song in history.

**2005**  Grammy Award: Lifetime Achievement Award; VH1: Led Zeppelin #1 on its list of 100 Greatest Artists of Hard Rock; *Guitar World*: Jimmy's solo in "Stairway to Heaven" as the greatest guitar solo in all rock history; Jimmy is awarded the Order of the British Empire.

**2006**  Led Zeppelin is awarded the Polar Music Prize; inducted into the UK Music Hall of Fame; *Guitar World*: Led Zeppelin declared the "world's greatest band."

**2007**  Grammy Hall of Fame: "Whole Lotta Love" is inducted into the Grammy Hall of Fame.

## Books

Bonham, Mick. *John Bonham: The Powerhouse Behind Led Zeppelin.* Harpenden, U.K.: Oldcastle Ltd., 2005.

Friend, Thomas W. *Fallen Angel: The Untold Story of Jimmy Page and Led Zeppelin.* Pittsburgh, Pa.: Gabriel, 2002.

Hoskyns, Barney. *Led Zeppelin IV.* Emmaus, Pa.: Rodale, 2006.

Lewis, Dave, and Paul Kendall. *Led Zeppelin: Talking.* London: Omnibus Press, 2004.

Shadwick, Keith. *Led Zeppelin: The Story of a Band and Their Music, 1968–1980.* San Francisco, Calif.: Backbeat Books, 2005.

Welch, Chris. *Led Zeppelin: Dazed and Confused, The Stories Behind Every Song.* New York: Avalon Publishing Group, 2006.

Welch, Chris, and Geoff Nicholls. *John Bonham: A Thunder of Drums.* San Francisco, Calif.: Backbeat Books, 2001.

## Web Sites

**www.jimmypageonline.com**
  Jimmy Page Online

**www.johnpauljones.com**
  John Paul Jones

**www.led-zeppelin.com**
  Led Zeppelin Official Site

**www.led-zeppelin.com/johnbonham**
  John Bonham

**www.robertplant.com**
  Robert Plant

**www.stryder.de**
  Led Zeppelin Live

**accolades**—Signs of high praise.

**acoustic**—Music that is not electronically amplified.

**allegations**—Assertions that are not proven or supported by evidence.

**antithetical**—The complete opposite of something.

**asphyxiated**—Suffocated.

**British Invasion**—The popularity and influence of British rock groups in the United States during the 1960s.

**criteria**—Standards for judging things.

**dynamic**—Active and changing.

**homage**—A show of reverence toward someone.

**obscurity**—The state of being unknown.

**platinum**—Signifying that an album or CD has sold two million copies, or a single has sold one million copies.

**savvy**—Shrewdness.

**synonymous**—Having the same meaning.

**synthesizers**—Electronic devices that create and modify sounds.

**venues**—Locations.

**vogue**—In style.

**waned**—Lessen.

**Ethan Schlesinger** is a musician and author. Originally from the Midwest, he now lives in New York.

## Picture Credits

page

**2:** Feature Image Archive
**8:** Bob Strong/AFP
**11:** New Millennium Images
**12:** UPI Photo Archive
**14:** Atlantic Records/Star Photos
**17:** EMI Records/Star Photos
**19:** Pictorial Press
**20:** Rex Features
**23:** Atlantic Records/Star Photos
**24:** Rex Features
**26:** Mirrorpix
**29:** Foto Feature Collection
**31:** Icon Image Express

**32:** Icon Image Express
**35:** Rex Features
**36:** New Millennium Images
**38:** Icon Image Express
**41:** New Millennium Images
**43:** Rex Features
**44:** New Millennium Images
**46:** New Millennium Images
**49:** UPI Photo Archive
**51:** Splash News
**52:** Sipa Press Photos
**54:** Philadelphia Inquirer/KRT

**Front cover:** Atlantic Records/Star Photos